DC™

SUPER-PETS!

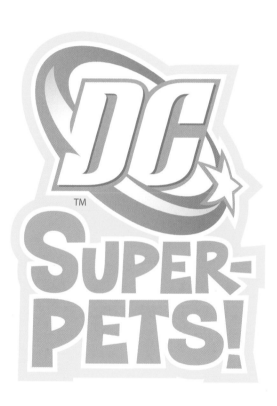

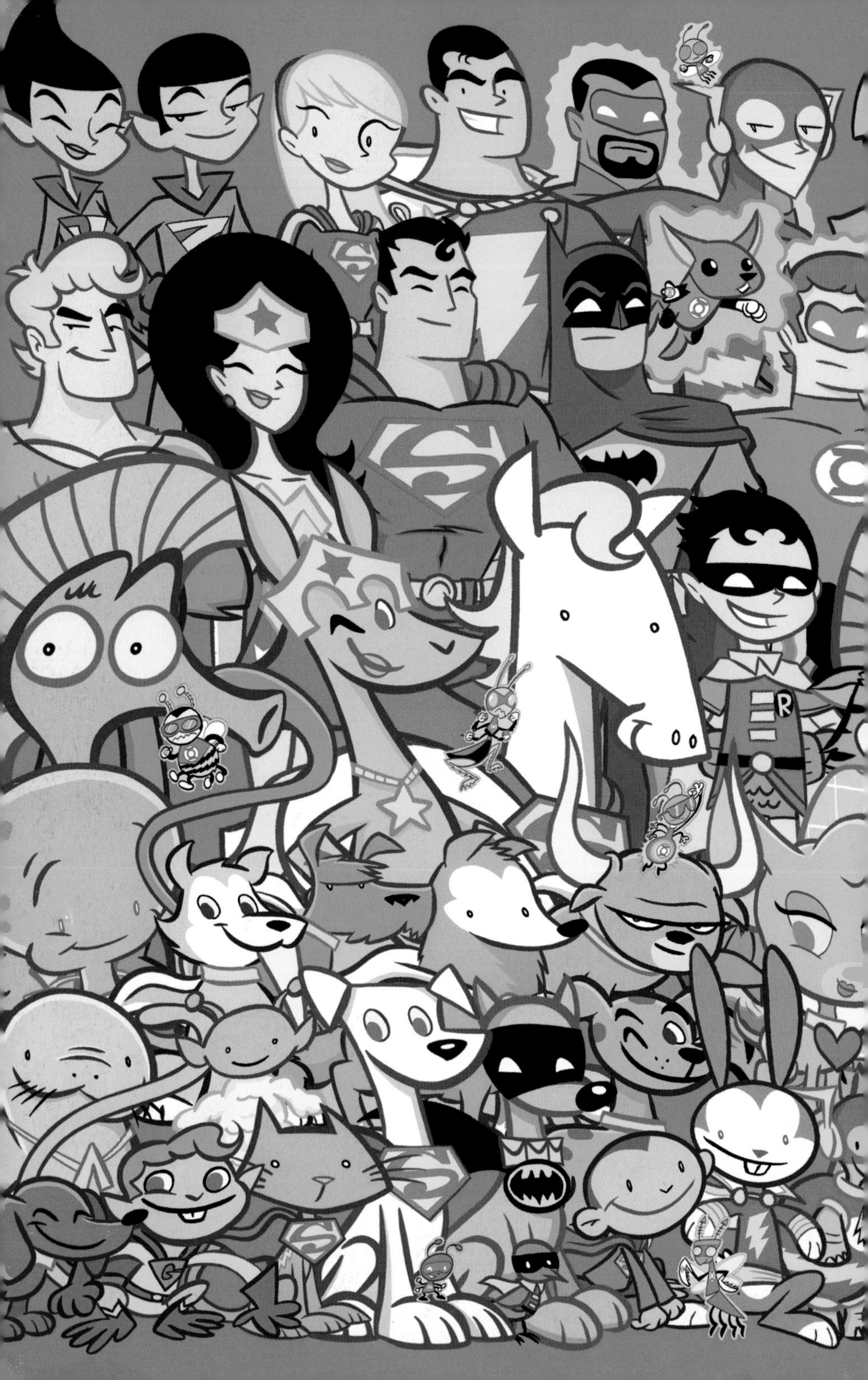

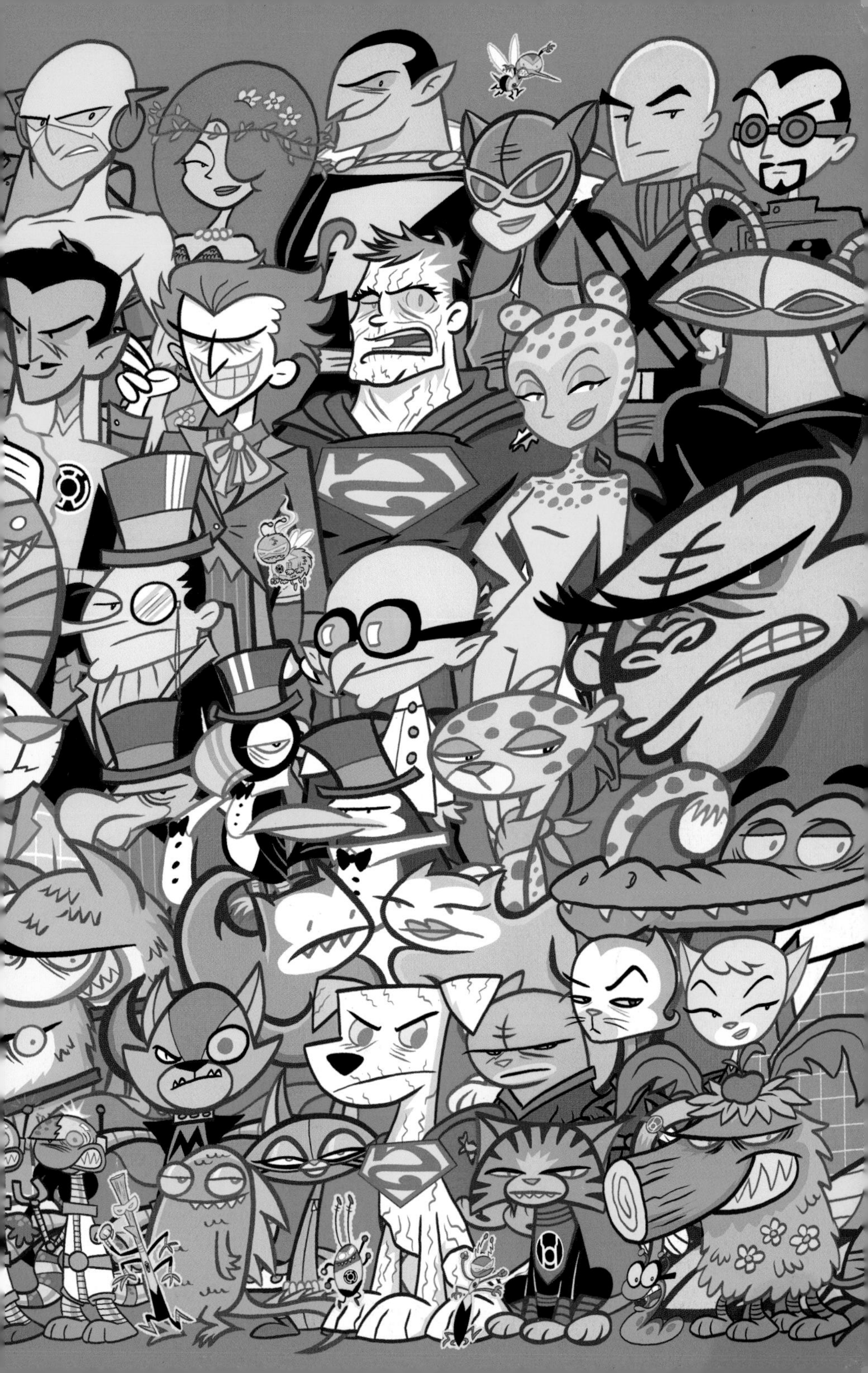

DC™

SUPER-PETS!

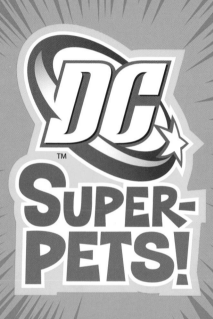

by Jane B. Mason

BATTLE BUGS
OF
OUTER SPACE

illustrated by
Art Baltazar

PICTURE WINDOW BOOKS
a capstone imprint

Starring...

BZZD
THE GREEN LANTERN!

GREEN LANTERN BUG CORPS!

SINESTRO BUG CORPS!

TABLE OF CONTENTS!

SUPER-PET HERO FILE 011:
GREEN LANTERN BUG CORPS

Bio: With their superpowered rings, the Green Lantern Bug Corps guards the universe and protects it from evil.

Gratch
Species: Mantis

Bzzd
Species: Space Bug

Eeny
Species: Ant

Zhoomp
Species: Grasshopper

Buzzoo
Species: Bee

Fossfur
Species: Firefly

Super Hero Pal:
JOHN STEWART
Green Lantern,
Space Sector 2814

SUPER-PET ENEMY FILE 011:
SINESTRO BUG CORPS

Eezix
Species: Mosquito

Tootz
Species: Stink Bug

Bio: The creepy crawly critters of the Sinestro Bug Corps use their yellow rings to spread fear across the universe.

Donald
Species: Cockroach

Webbik
Species: Tarantula

Waxxee
Species: Earwig

Fimble
Species: Stick Insect

Super-villain Pal:
SINESTRO
**Leader of Sinestro Corps
Base:** Qward

PEST CRIME

CRAAAAACK!

The baseball soared into left field

at Coast City Stadium. The batter

dropped his bat and ran to first base.

"**Yay!**" Bzzd shouted. "**Go, go, go!**"

His wings flapped wildly. He watched

number 38 head toward second base.

Bzzd loved baseball. He was having a great time at the ballpark on Earth. The sun was shining. The fans were cheering. And the Rockets, his favorite team, were winning!

Bzzd was not your average baseball fan. He wasn't even human! He was an insect. More importantly, he was a member of the Green Lantern Corps.

Using powerful rings, the Green Lanterns protected the universe from evildoers. This giant-sized job rarely left Bzzd time to relax.

"**Go, go, go!**" Bzzd shouted again. He zoomed behind the pitcher for a better view of the action.

The next Rockets player was up to bat. The pitcher from the other team, the Warriors, looked mad. Who could blame him? His team was losing 6–2 in the bottom of the seventh inning. Time was running out.

The batter stepped up to the plate.

Strike one! Strike two! Then the pitcher

hurled another fastball, and the batter

swung for a third time.

"A roach! A roach!" someone

suddenly screamed in the stands.

"It's a hit!" the announcer shouted.

Bzzd wanted to watch the play. But as a **Green Lantern**, he knew that duty called. He soared into the stands to check out the screams.

"Help me! Help me!" a woman yelled at the top of her lungs.

Bzzd hovered over the woman's shoulder. Sure enough, a giant cockroach was crawling all over her jumbo hot dog. And not just any cockroach, either. It was **Donald!**

Bzzd and Donald had crossed paths before. Donald was a member of the evil **Sinestro Bug Corps**. He liked to stir up trouble. The roach smiled and took a bite out of the lady's hot dog.

Bzzd scowled.

Hot dogs were a big part of baseball.
Fans were supposed to be able to enjoy
them at games.

Donald rubbed his legs together
greedily. He took another bite.

FWOOOOSH!

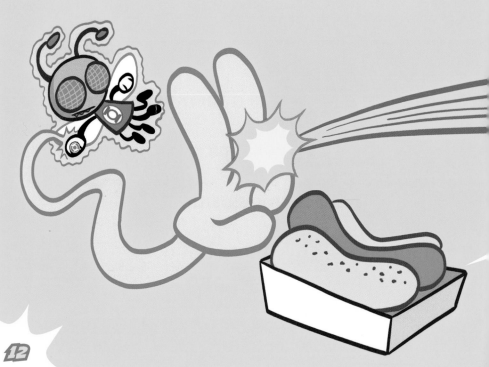

Bzzd's power ring flashed, shooting a ray of green energy. He imagined a finger flicking Donald off the hot dog.

THWIP! Half a second later, Donald was squirming on his back on the stadium floor.

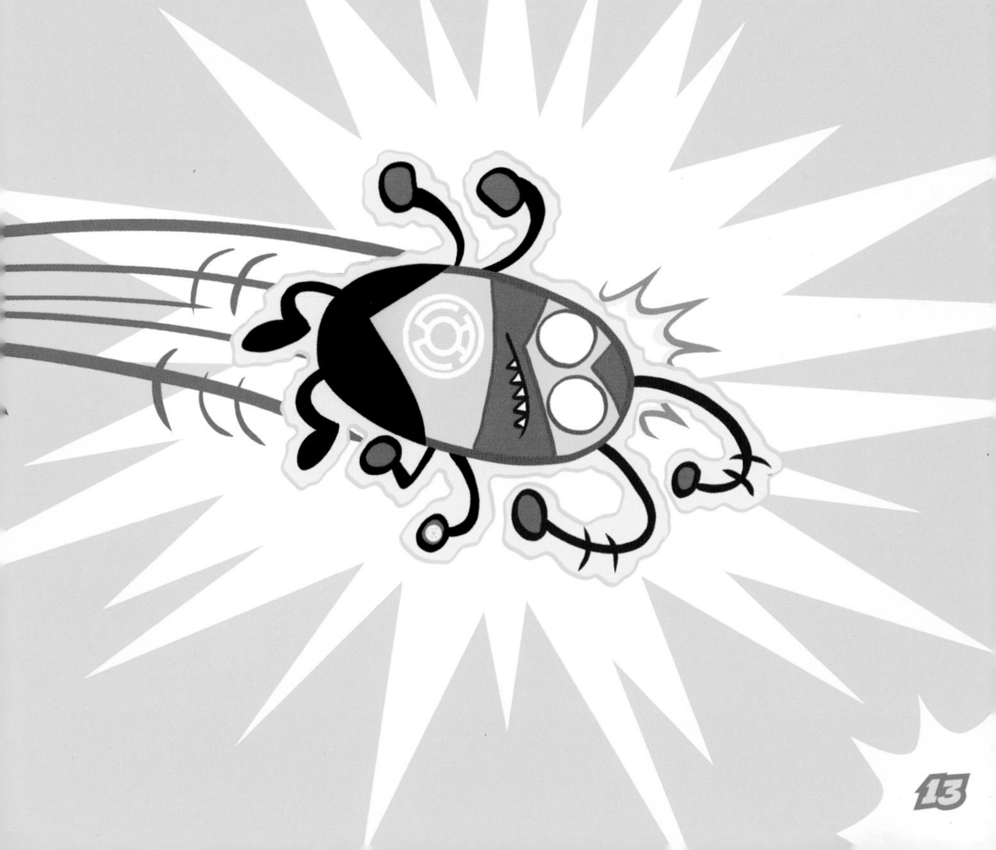

"Hey!" shouted the roach.

BWEEOOM!

Yellow light shot out of Donald's

ring, knocking Bzzd off balance.

Donald tackled Bzzd in midair, and the

two fell to the ground in a heap.

"If you want a hot dog, get your

own," Bzzd said calmly. He wriggled

himself free and took a step back.

"Mind your business!" said Donald.

"Yeah, mind your own business,"

said a second voice.

Bzzd spotted **Webbik**, a Sinestro spider, staring at him from an empty seat. Webbik was a tarantula with a tiny brain and knack for trouble.

"You're no match for us, you winged weakling!" Webbik snorted.

"Warriors rule!" Donald added.

Bzzd knew he should ignore their insults. He also knew he had to stand up to the bug bullies!

"Is that why the Warriors are eating the Rockets' dust?" Bzzd replied.

Bzzd saw a flash of anger in the eyes of the evil bugs. A second later, their rings began firing in all directions. If these villains weren't stopped, America's pastime would soon become the world's worst pest crime!

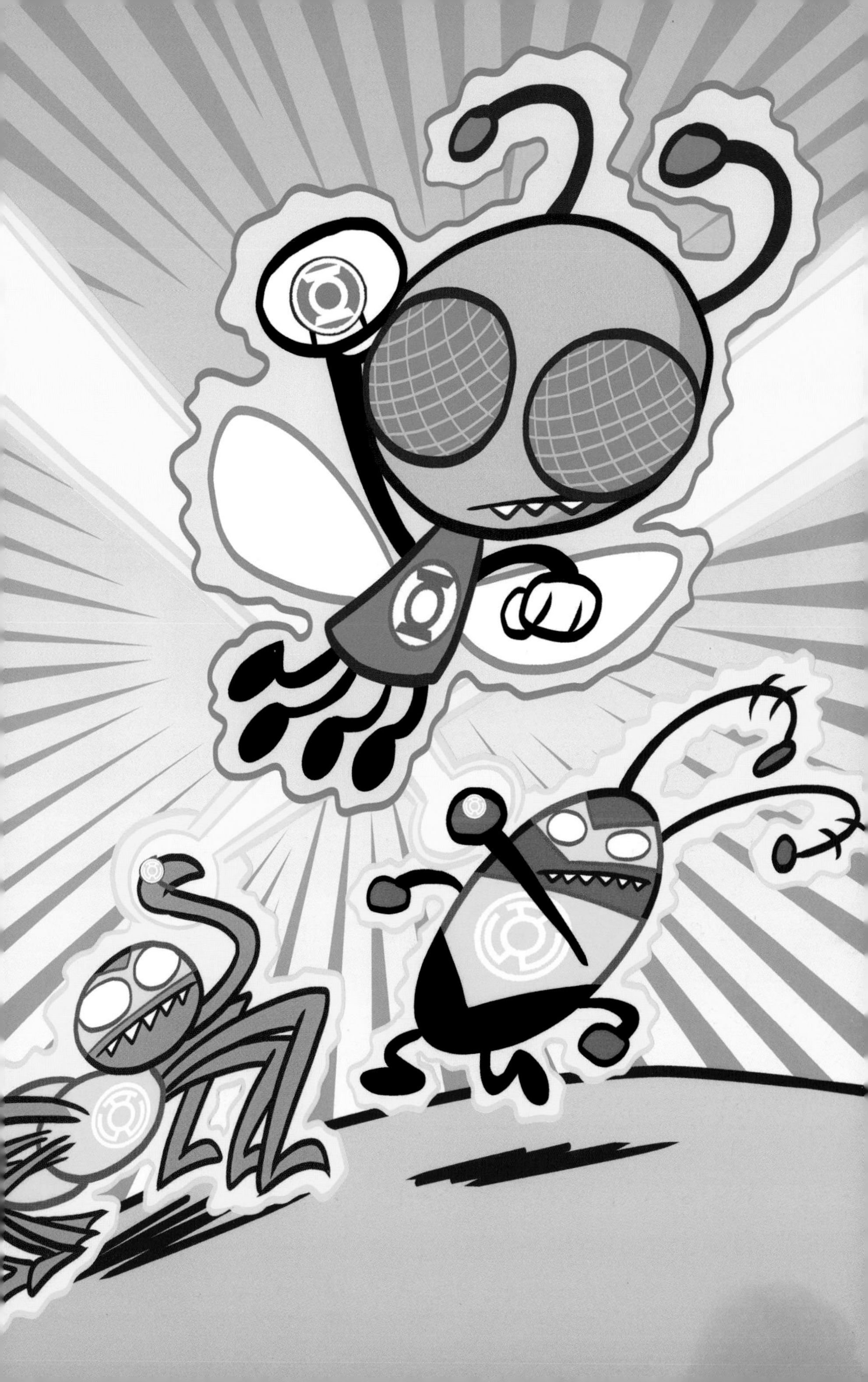

Chapter 2

IT'S A HIT!

Bzzd was no scaredy-bug, but he was no fool, either. He took off as fast as his vibrating wings could carry him.  The sound of his beating wings hummed in his ears. He rounded third base and headed for the pitcher's mound.

Donald and Webbik were behind him. Their yellow rings continued to blast rays of light. **BWEEOOM!**

Meanwhile, the game was in the top of the eighth inning. The Warriors were up at bat. The first pitch sailed across the plate. The batter swung.

"Strike one!" yelled the umpire.

Bzzd darted toward the Rockets' dugout. A beam of yellow light behind him got closer and closer.

"Zap him!" Donald shouted.

A wild yellow light shot out of Webbik's ring and blasted Bzzd. The Green Lantern felt dizzy. **He couldn't fly straight!**

Up ahead, a row of Warriors sat on the bench, waiting for their turn at bat. Player number 43 took off his baseball cap to scratch his head. Bzzd tried to steer clear, but the whole world was yellow and spinning!

 He buzzed frantically.

Oof! Too late. Bzzd had already landed in a giant head of curly hair.

"Ah! Get it out! Get it out!" shouted player number 43. "There's something in my hair!"

Webbik and Donald roared with laughter as number 43 swiped at his head. He nearly squashed Bzzd flat.

Bzzd focused on his ring. He shot out an arc of green energy. Then he soared out of the sweaty tangles like a jet.

Bzzd glanced over his shoulder. The Sinestro Corps duo crashed into a giant pole at the edge of the dugout. They fell to the dirt floor in a tangle of spider and roach legs.

Bzzd smirked and headed toward home plate. The baseball game was still in the eighth inning. The score was still 6–2. The Warriors had two outs, and the batter had two strikes.

"Looks like it's do or die for your team!" said Bzzd.

"I couldn't have said it better **myself!"** Donald shouted back above the roar of the crowd. He shot another beam of yellow light at Bzzd.

The pitcher wound up. The ball sailed toward home. Bzzd heard it coming and tried to dodge, but the yellow light held him back. Donald and Webbik crashed into him, and the ball smashed into all three bugs.

The Warriors' batter struck the ball hard, sending it flying.

"Whoooaaa!" the threesome cried. The baseball — and the bugs — sailed over the stands and out of the park.

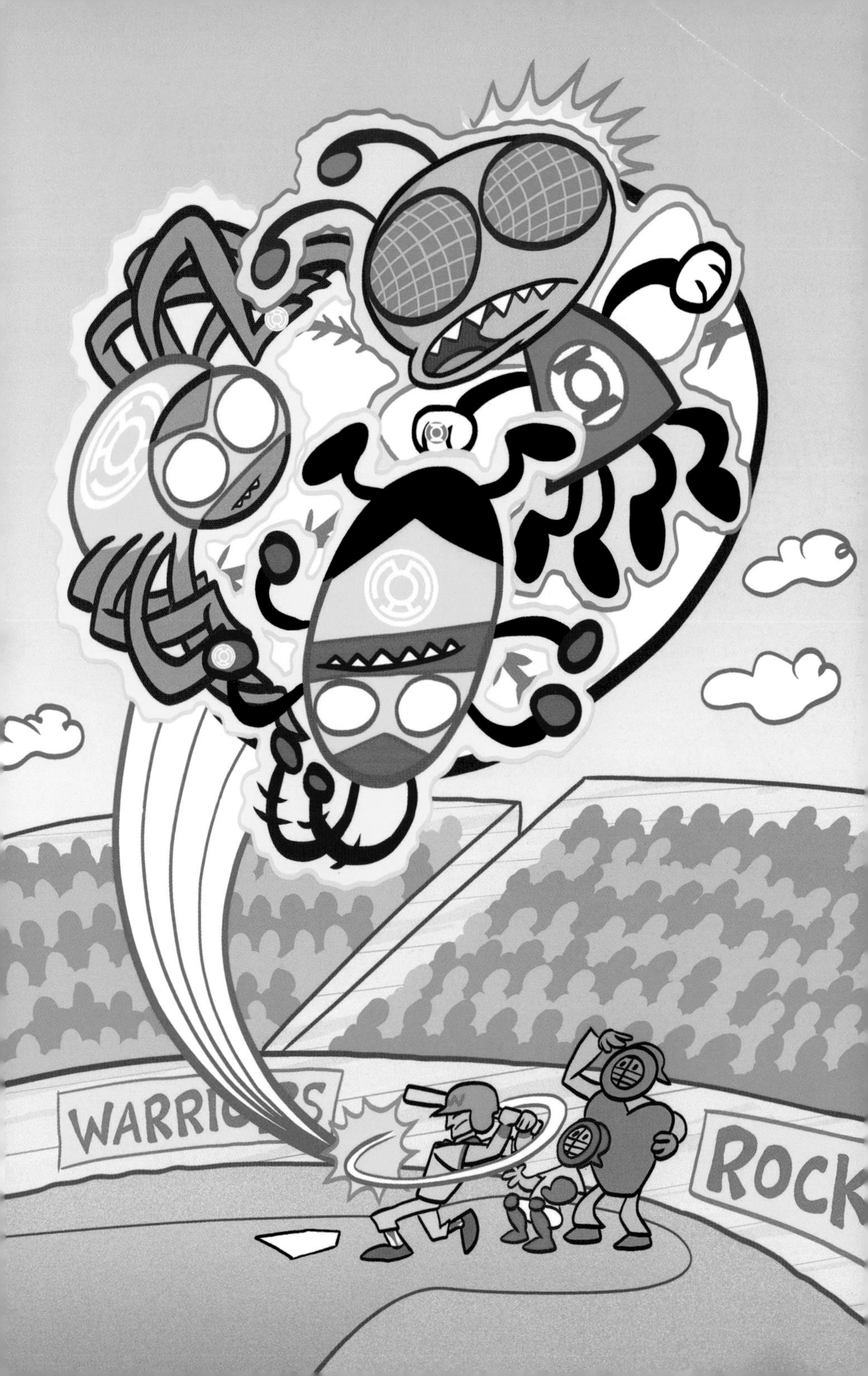

WARRIORS
ROCK

WHAM!!!

The bugs landed in a stinky

dumpster behind the ballpark.

"Where are we?" Bzzd asked.

"In heaven!" Donald cried out.

Bzzd looked around. **"Heaven?"** he

repeated.

"Yes, heaven," Donald confirmed.

"A giant pile of garbage!"

Bzzd wiggled his antennae in the

air. It did smell pretty good.

"Lunchtime!" Donald cried. He crawled over to a half-eaten pretzel covered with mustard slime.

"I'm a little hungry myself," Webbik said, sniffing some moldy peanuts.

Bzzd started to bite into an old hot dog. **FIZZZZL!!**

A beam of energy suddenly struck him in the back. "Ouch!" he yelled.

"Back off, mangy maggot!" shouted Donald. He pointed his power ring toward Bzzd. "This garbage is ours!"

"Yeah!" Webbik agreed. "And don't try anything funny. **We've got you outnumbered!"**

WHOOSH! Just then, a neon light flashed through the dumpster.

The Green Lantern firefly, **Fossfur**, suddenly landed next to Bzzd. "Beep! Wrong," he said, blinking his tail on and off. "I believe the score is tied."

"Ha! Think again!" shouted Donald.

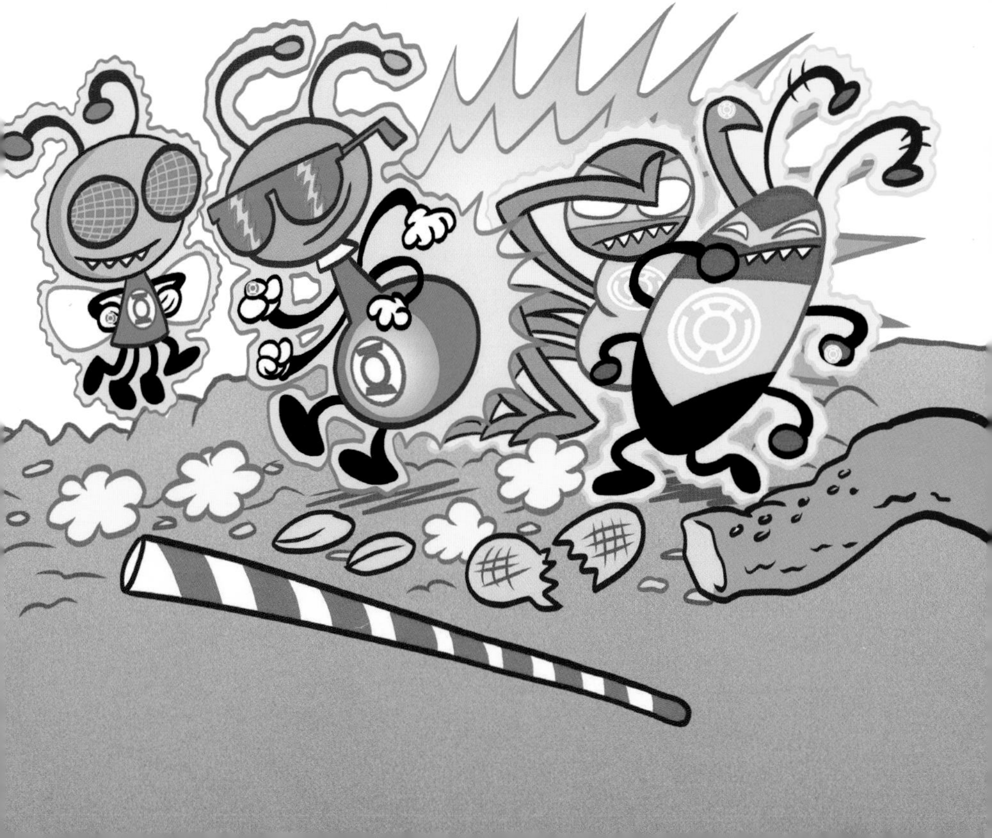

The dumpster started shaking like an earthquake. It rocked side to side and up and down. Then, from beneath the piles of gooey garbage, **other Sinestro Corps Bugs appeared**. Each one carried its own yellow ring.

"It's game over for you two," said Donald. The rotten roach pointed his power ring at the Green Lanterns. The other evil insects followed his lead.

"Beep! Wrong again," Fossfur said. "This bug battle has just begun!"

BUG BATTLE

Bzzd and Fossfur held their power rings into the air. Together, they repeated the Green Lantern oath:

"In brightest day, in blackest night, no evil shall escape my sight. Let those who worship evil's might, beware my power — Green Lantern's light!"

Bzzd and Fossfur each imagined a giant can of bug spray. A second later, the objects appeared from their rings. The Green Lanterns pointed the cans at the bad news bugs and blasted them with a mighty mist of energy.

The Sinestro Corps Bugs starting coughing and falling down.

"Phew!" shouted Donald the roach, trying to fan away the mist with his tiny legs. "That's a rotten thing to do!"

"Did someone say rotten?" asked **Tootz**, another Sinestro Bug, from nearby. "They don't call me a stink bug for nothing!" The smelly bug let out an awful odor of his own.

Bzzd and Fossfur couldn't handle the stench. They created a stink-proof bubble with their rings and hid inside.

The Sinestro Corps Bugs surrounded them. "Looks like you're caught in a pickle," said Donald the roach. "Are you ready to give up?"

Fossfur the firefly blinked his behind on and off. On and off. On and off.

"Is he surrendering?" Donald asked the evil mosquito next to him.

"Don't ask me!" said Eezix. "I don't speak glow bug."

"He's not giving up," shouted Bzzd. "He's calling in our relievers!"

Suddenly, four more Green Lantern insects dived into the dumpster. They shot glowing green baseballs at Donald and the other Sinestro Bugs.

"Bet you didn't see that curveball coming," joked Bzzd with a laugh.

KA-POW! KA-POW!

He fired two glowing green stingers

at the rotten roach. He missed.

"Haha!" Donald exclaimed. "That's

two strikes. One more, and you're out!"

He held out his ring and returned fire.

On the far side of the dumpster, **Eeny** the ant faced off against the Sinestro stick insect. Fimble was more than twice the Green Lantern's size.

"Ha! It's not even fair," said Fimble, laughing at the teensy ant. "I'll snap this puny pest like a twig!"

"Let's see if YOU like being picked on," shouted Eeny. **"Or should I say pecked on?"** The ant created a giant woodpecker with his ring. It chased after the stick insect like a tasty treat.

Meanwhile, the other insect enemies

shot beams of green and yellow light

back and forth at each other.

BEEOOM! BEEOOM!

The dingy dumpster quickly turned

into a critter cage match.

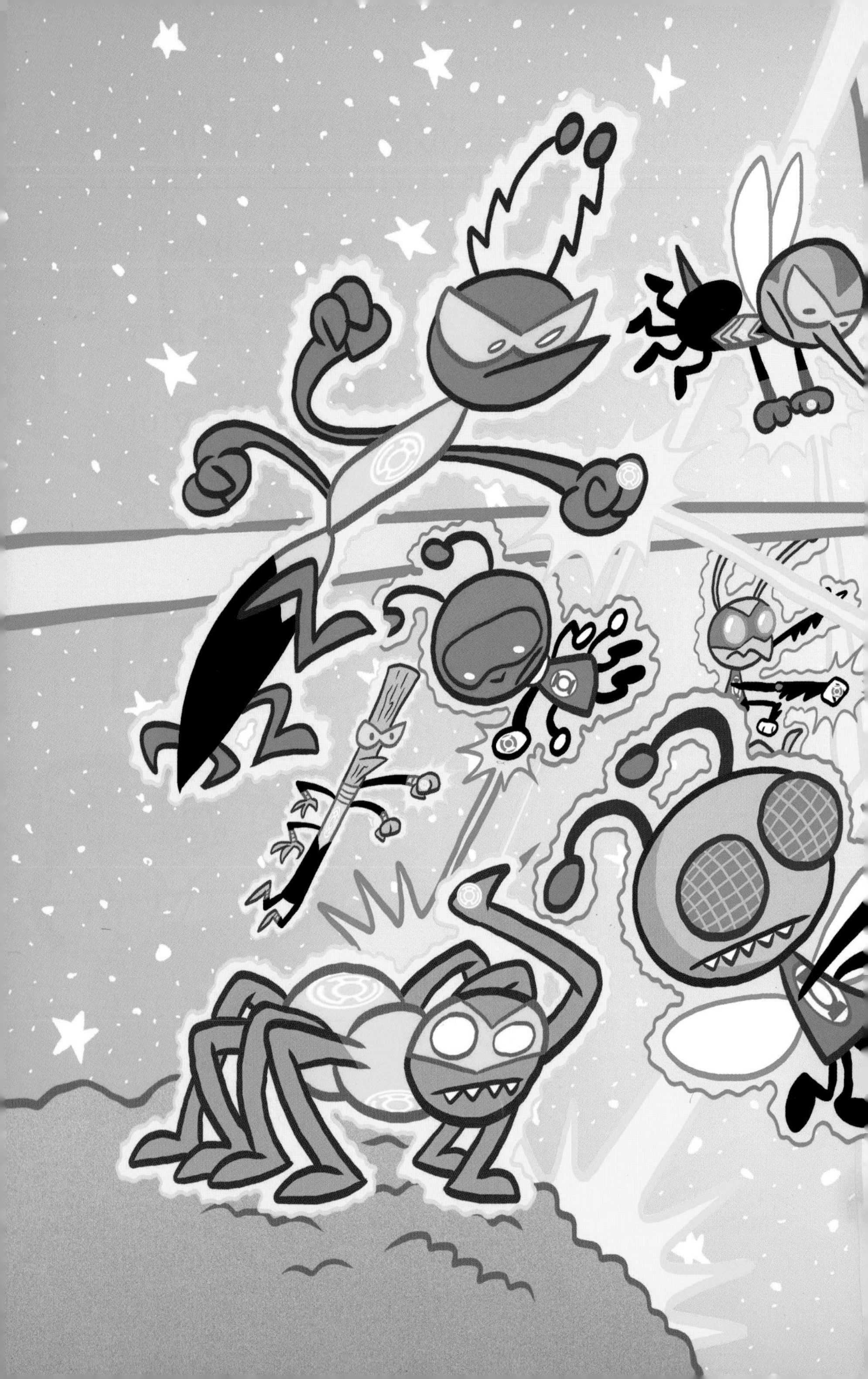

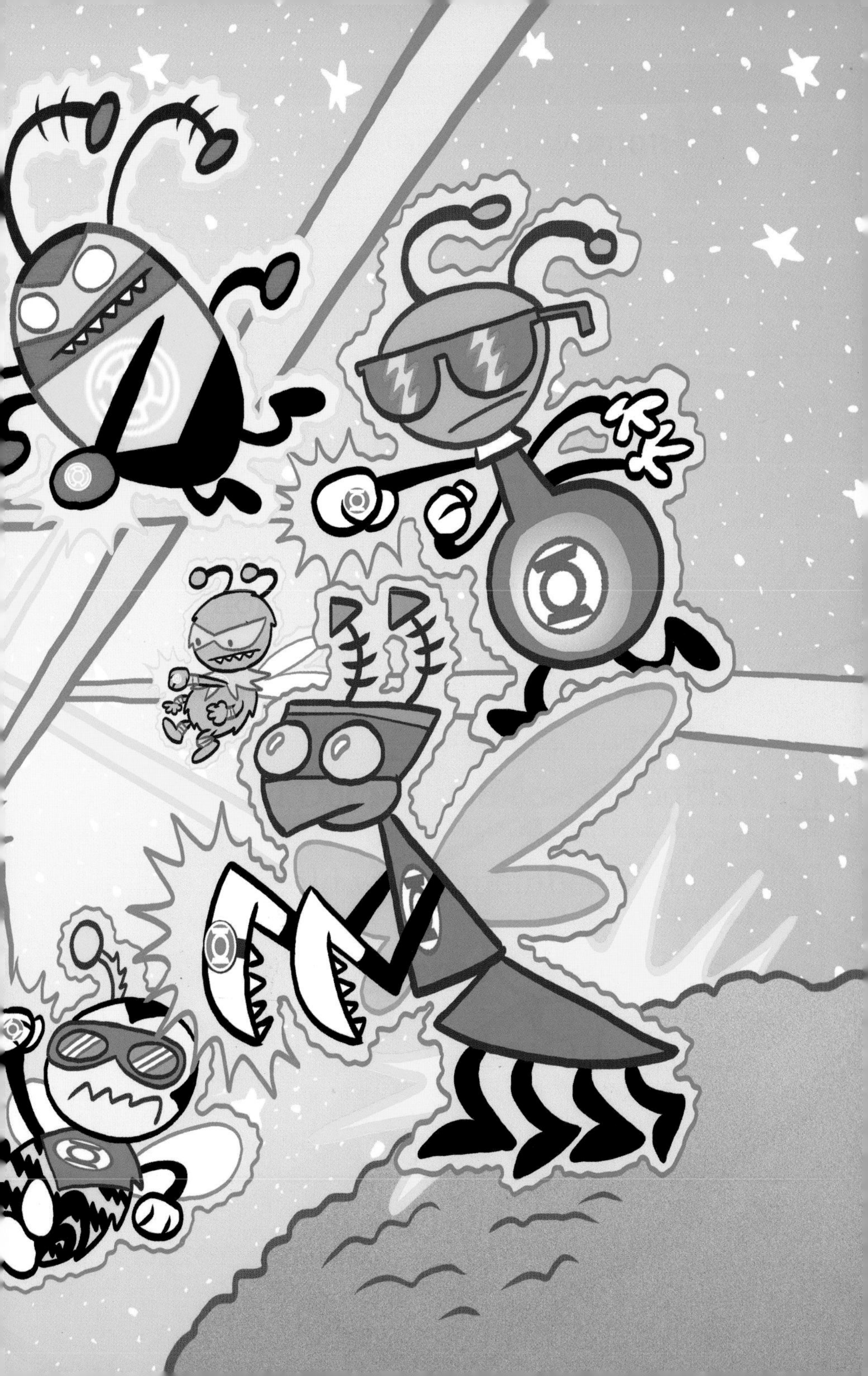

"Give up!" said Donald the roach. "You're no match for our pest powers!"

Fossfur started blinking again.

"Now what?!" asked Donald.

The firefly pointed to the sky. His tail blinked faster and faster.

"Listen," said Waxee the earwig. "I think I hear something." The Green Lantern bug looked up, and the other pests followed his gaze.

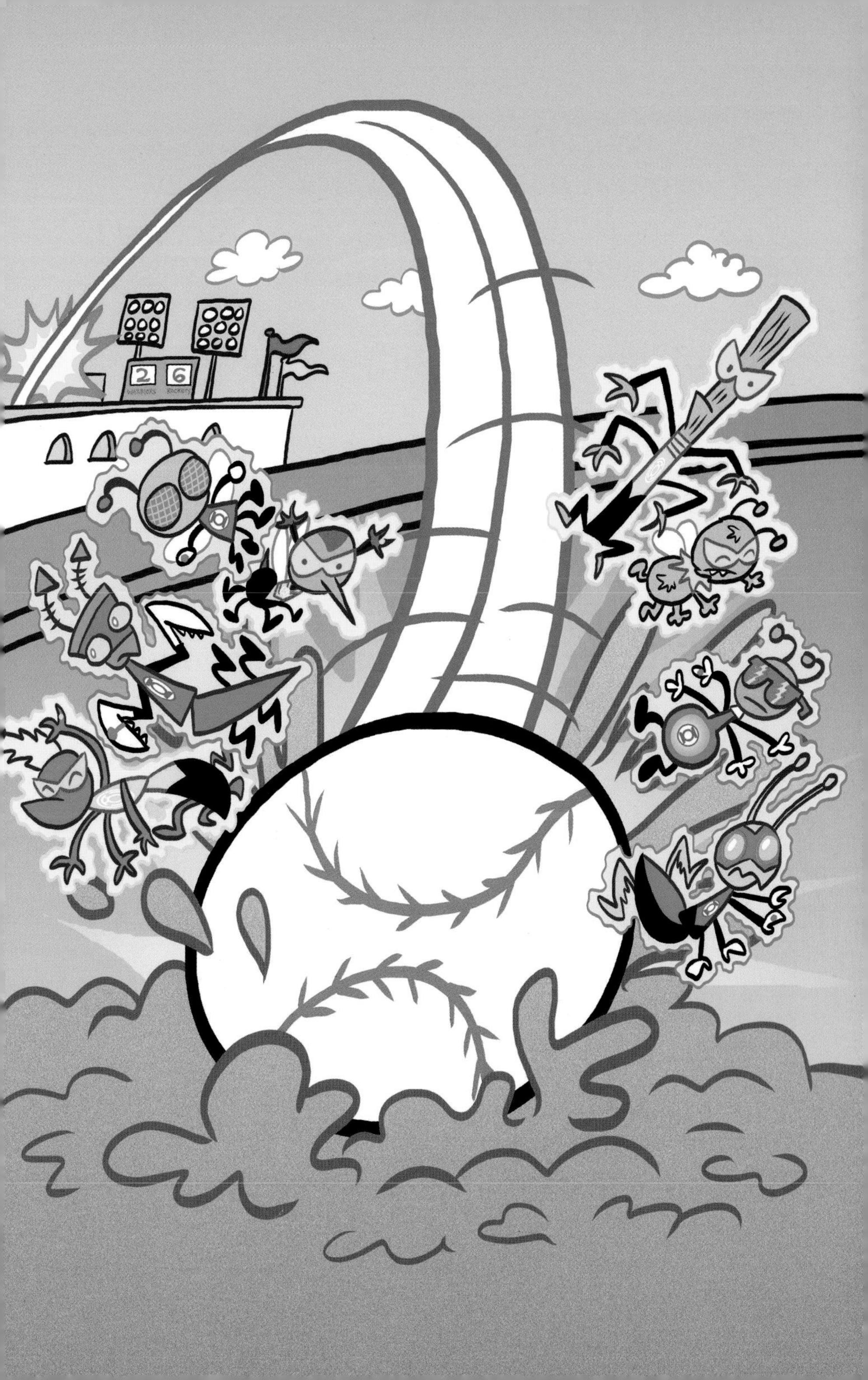
2
6

A giant baseball fell from the sky like a two-ton bomb. The insects flew in all directions, nearly squashed by the massive orb.

"Who did that?" said Donald.

Lying on the floor, Bzzd suddenly remembered the baseball game. He flew to the top of the dumpster and looked out. The stadium scoreboard read 6–6 in the bottom of the ninth inning. The Warriors had just tied the game with a mighty grand slam.

"Ha!" Donald exclaimed. He and the other bugs had crawled up beside Bzzd. "Looks like this game isn't over."

"Neither is this bug battle," said Bzzd. **"But for now, how about we call it a tie?"**

The other bugs agreed.

"Besides," added Bzzd, "you know

what extra innings means, right?"

The bugs looked out at the stadium.

Thousands of hungry fans munched

on hot dogs, popcorn, and peanuts.

Fossfur blinked his tail. Tootz the stink bug let out a giant burp. Webbik the tarantula licked his hairy lips.

"Extra garbage!" Donald exclaimed.

"Exactly," said Bzzd, leading them toward the stands. "Play ball!"

KNOW YOUR HERO PETS!

1. Krypto
2. Streaky
3. Beppo
4. Comet
5. Ace
6. Robin Robin
7. Jumpa
8. Whatzit
9. Storm
10. Topo
11. Ark
12. Hoppy
13. Batcow
14. Big Ted
15. Proty
16. Gleek
17. Paw Pooch
18. Bull Dog
19. Chameleon Collie
20. Hot Dog
21. Tail Terrier
22. Tusky Husky
23. Mammoth Mutt
24. Dawg
25. B'dg
26. Stripezoid
27. Zallion
28. Ribitz
29. Bzzd
30. Gratch
31. Buzzoo
32. Fossfur
33. Zhoomp
34. Eeny

1

2

3

4

5

6

7

8

9

10

11

12

13

14

15

16

17

18

19

20

21

22

23

24

25

26

27

28

29

30

31

32

33

34

KNOW YOUR VILLAIN PETS!

1. Bizarro Krypto
2. Ignatius
3. Rozz
4. Mechanikat
5. Crackers
6. Giggles
7. Joker Fish
8. Chauncey
9. Artie Puffin
10. Griff
11. Waddles
12. Dogwood
13. Mr. Mind
14. Sobek
15. Misty
16. Sneezers
17. General Manx
18. Nizz
19. Fer-El
20. Titano
21. Bit-Bit
22. X-43
23. Dex-Starr
24. Glomulus
25. Whoosh
26. Pronto
27. Snorrt
28. Rolf
29. Tootz
30. Eezix
31. Donald
32. Waxxee
33. Fimble
34. Webbik

1

2

3

4

5

6

7

8

9

10

11

12

13

14

15

16

17

18

19

20

21

22

23

24

25

26

27

28

29

30

31

32

33

34

AW YEAH, JOKES!

What do you call a fly with no wings?

No idea.

A walk!

What do you call spiders that just got married?

Tell me.

Newlywebs!

Why was the mother firefly happy?

Tell me.

Because her children were all so bright!

WORD POWER!

antennae (an-TEN-nay)—the feelers on the head of an insect

corps (KOR)—a group of creatures acting together or doing the same thing

dugout (DUHG-out)—a shelter where baseball players sit when they are not at bat or in the field

maggot (MAG-uht)—the larva of certain flies

oath (OHTH)—a serious, formal promise

pastime (PASS-time)—a hobby or sports activity that makes time pass in an enjoyable way

tarantula (tuh-RAN-chuh-luh)—a large, hairy spider found mainly in warm regions

universe (YOO-nuh-vurss)—the Earth, the planets, the stars, and all things that exist in space

MEET THE AUTHOR!

Jane B. Mason

Jane Mason is no super hero, but having three kids sometimes makes her wish she had superpowers. Jane has written children's books for more than fifteen years and hopes to continue doing so for fifty more. She makes her home in Oakland, California, with her husband, three children, their dog, and a gecko.

MEET THE ILLUSTRATOR!

Eisner Award-winner Art Baltazar

Art Baltazar is a cartoonist machine from the heart of Chicago! He defines cartoons and comics not only as an art style, but as a way of life. Currently, Art is the creative force behind *The New York Times* best-selling, Eisner Award-winning, DC Comics series Tiny Titans, and the co-writer for *Billy Batson and the Magic of SHAZAM!* Art is living the dream! He draws comics and never has to leave the house. He lives with his lovely wife, Rose, big boy Sonny, little boy Gordon, and little girl Audrey. Right on!

READ THEM ALL!

DC SUPER-PETS!

THE FUN DOESN'T STOP HERE!

Discover more:

- Videos & Contests!
- Games & Puzzles!
- Heroes & Villains!
- Authors & Illustrators!

@ www.capstonekids.com

Find cool websites and more books like this one
at www.facthound.com Just type in Book I.D.
9781404864825 and you're ready to go!

PICTURE WINDOW BOOKS
a capstone imprint

Published in 2013
A Capstone Imprint
1710 Roe Crest Drive
North Mankato, MN 56003
www.capstonepub.com

Copyright © 2013 DC Comics.
DC SUPER-PETS and all related characters and
elements © & ™ DC Comics.
(s13)

STAR13055

All rights reserved. No part of this publication may
be reproduced in whole or in part, or stored in a
retrieval system, or transmitted in any form or by
any means, electronic, mechanical, photocopying,
recording, or otherwise, without written permission.

Cataloging-in-Publication Data is available
at the Library of Congress website.
ISBN: 978-1-4048-6482-5 (library binding)
ISBN: 978-1-4048-6848-9 (paperback)

Summary: The evil Sinestro Bug Corps
have invaded a baseball game on Earth.
Thankfully, the Green Lantern Bug Corps
are out to stop them! If they don't, America's
favorite pastime might become the world's
worst pest crime.

Art Director & Designer: Bob Lentz
Editor: Donald Lemke
Creative Director: Heather Kindseth
Editorial Director: Michael Dahl

Printed and bound in the USA.
072018   000757

DC™

SUPER-PETS!

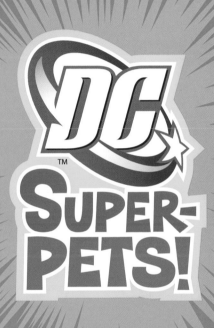

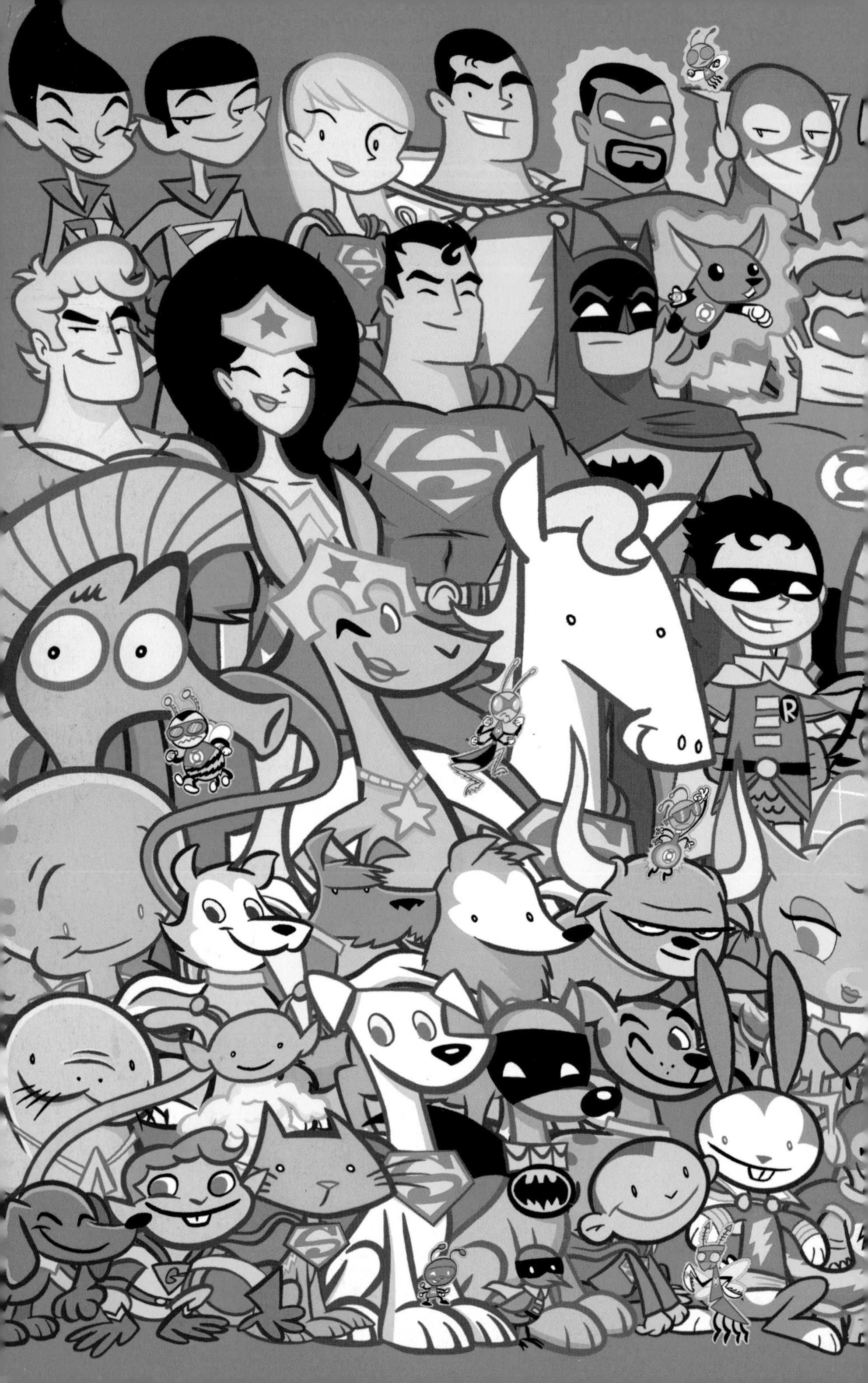

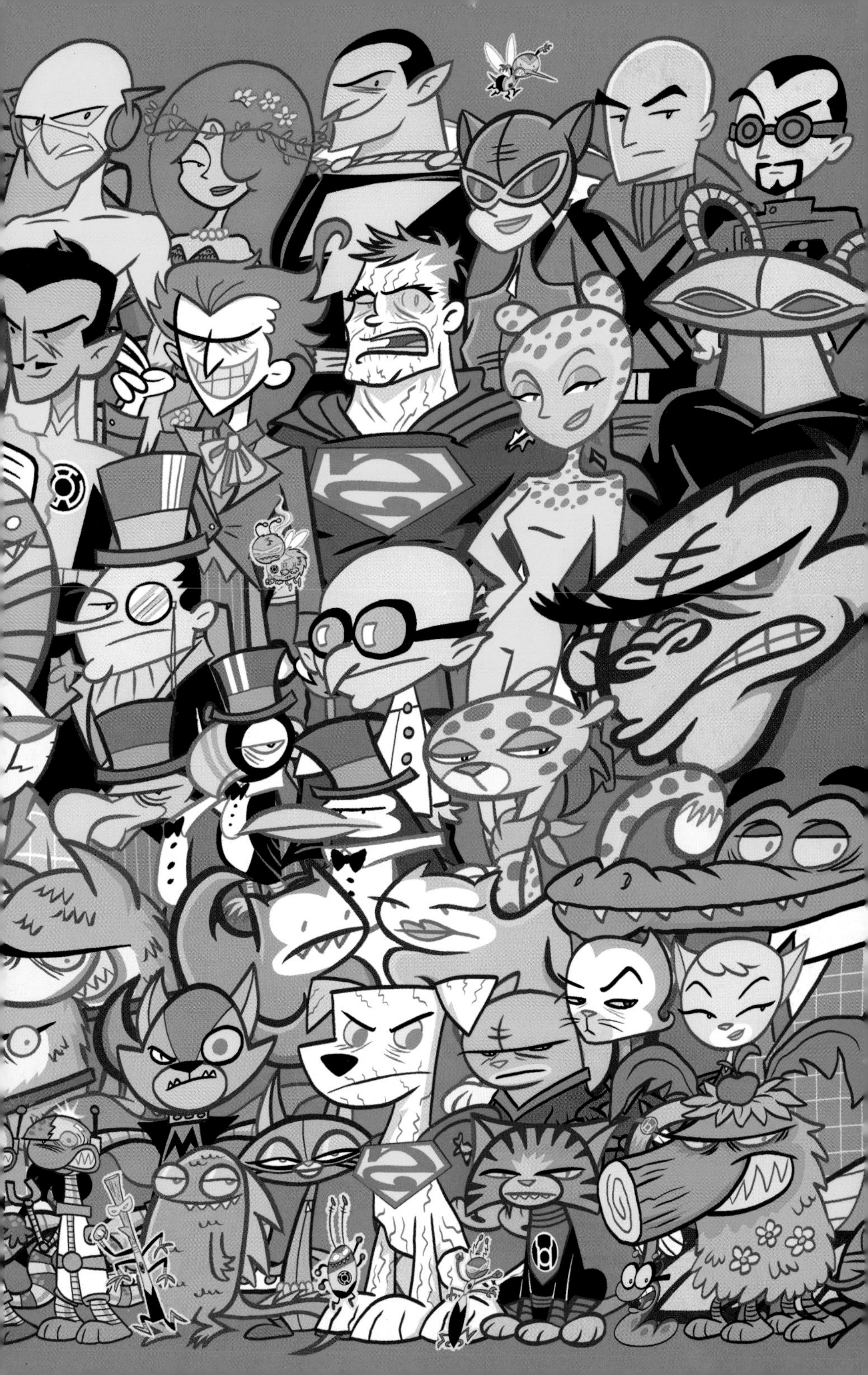

DC™

SUPER-PETS!

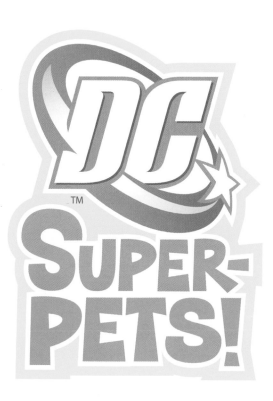